Town Mouse and Country Mouse

Illustrated by Eric Kincaid

SHOOTING STAR PRESS

Once there were two mice.
One mouse lived in a house in the
middle of a town. He was called
the town mouse.

The second mouse lived in the
country. His house was on the edge
of a field. He was called the
country mouse.

The town mouse and the country
mouse met one day at a wedding.
They soon became friends.

One day the
country mouse sent
a letter to the
town mouse.
It said, "Would
you like to come
and stay with me
in the country?"

The town mouse was
pleased. He had
never been to the
country. He packed
his bag. He went
to the country
the same day.

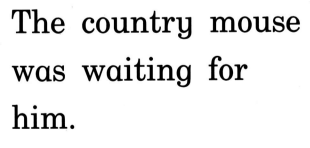

The country mouse
was waiting for
him.
"Please come in,"
said the country
mouse.

The country mouse showed the town mouse his house. It did not take long. His house was very small.

The country mouse liked his small house. It was cosy. The town mouse thought it a bit TOO small.

The country mouse got some food ready. There was barleycorn and roots. The country mouse had roots every day. Roots and barleycorn were the only food he had. He was used to them. He liked them.
The town mouse did not like them at all. He pulled a face.

The town mouse felt sorry for the country mouse. He would not like to live in a small house. He would not like to eat roots all the time. "Come to the town and stay with me," said the town mouse. "I will show you what good living is about."

The country mouse packed his bag.
He locked the door of his house.
Then he went to the town with the
town mouse.

The country mouse had never been to
the town. It was very busy.
They came to some steps.
"What a big house," said the
country mouse.
"This is where I live," said the
town mouse. "Come in."

The town mouse took the country mouse to the larder. The country mouse gasped. He had never seen so much food in one place. There was flour and oatmeal, figs and honey and dates.

"Help yourself," said the town mouse.
"Can I?" said the country mouse.
"Of course you can," said the town mouse. "Eat whatever you like."
The country mouse liked the look of the dates. He had never seen a date before. He sniffed it. It smelt good.

The country mouse nibbled at the date. He liked the taste. Suddenly the town mouse pricked up his ears.

"Quick!" said the town mouse. "Someone is coming. We must hide." The two mice ran and hid in a tiny hole.

They waited until it was safe to
come out. They seemed to wait a
long time. The country mouse did
not like hiding. He wanted to eat
that date. At last the town mouse
said it was safe to leave the hole.

The country mouse
finished the date.
He started to eat
a fig.
Suddenly the town
mouse pricked up
his ears.

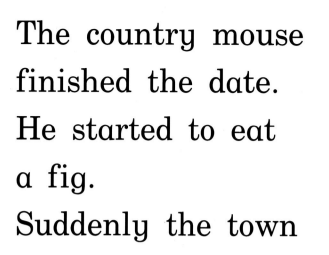

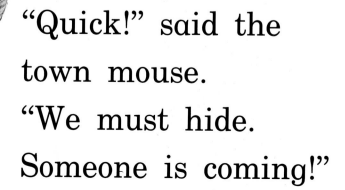

"Quick!" said the
town mouse.
"We must hide.
Someone is coming!"

The two mice hid again.
"Does this happen often?" asked the country mouse.
"Oh, all the time," said the town mouse. "You will soon get used to it."

"I do not want to get used to it," said the country mouse. "I do not like running to hide when I am eating. It makes my tummy ache. I am going home."

The country mouse was very glad to be home. He might have only roots to eat, but at least he could eat them in peace.

All these appear in the pages of
the story. Can you find them?

town mouse

country mouse

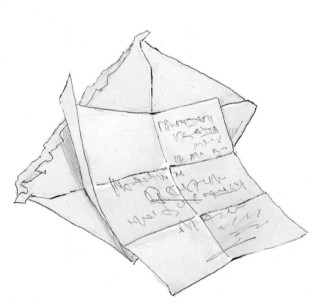

letter

barleycorn